Last Week

For Rowan and Justin:
Excellent Men, Masters of the House
— BR

Last Week

Written by
Bill Richardson

Illustrated by
Emilie Leduc

Afterword by
Dr. Stefanie Green

Groundwood Books
House of Anansi Press
Toronto / Berkeley

Seconds

In this last week there are seven days.

In those days there are one hundred and sixty-eight hours.

In those hours there are ten thousand and eighty minutes.

In those minutes there are six hundred four thousand and eight hundred seconds.

That's a lot of seconds. I wish there were more, but some things can't be changed. Six hundred four thousand and eight hundred seconds. Those are all the seconds any week, even a last week, can hold.

Monday

"Make every second count."

That's what Flippa says. We call my gran Flippa because every day, no matter the weather, she swims in the sea. She puts on her wetsuit, cap, goggles and flippers. She walks down to the beach. *Flippa-flop, flippa-flap.* Neighbors hear her as she travels the three blocks there and the three blocks back. *Flippa-flop, flippa-flap.* They smile and wave.

Flippa can't swim anymore. Her wetsuit hangs in the closet like a creepy rubber skin. Today, I put on her goggles and her flippers, and I walked into her bedroom.

"Boo!" I said.

She said, "Look who's come to call. It's the creature from the Black Lagoon."

"Who?" I asked, but before she could tell me the story, the phone rang. Again.

"I'll tell you later," she said.

But there's not much later left.

All that's left of later are five hundred eighteen thousand four hundred seconds.

Tuesday

Ring, ring, ring.
Ring, ring, ring.

If it's not the phone, it's the door buzzer. My job is to greet the visitors. I take their coats and hang them in the closet next to the wetsuit. If they've brought food, I take that, too. Almost everyone brings food. Brownies. Cheesecake. Banana bread. Casseroles.

"What army is going to come marching through to eat all this stuff?" my dad asks.

Flippa is Dad's mother. We flew clear across the country to be here for this last week. Mom stayed behind. She has to work. She'll come on Thursday.

Dad sleeps in the guest room, next to Flippa's bedroom. I sleep on the foldout couch, near the kitchen. Last night, I woke up. I saw Dad. He was standing in the light of the open fridge. He was staring at all that food. He wasn't making any sounds, but I could tell by the way his shoulders shook that he was crying.

I lay awake. I did the math. In four hundred and thirty-two thousand seconds, this last week will be over.

Wednesday

Dad cries. I cry. Visitors cry. We gush and gulp and sob. It's a sloppy business. No one seems embarrassed, though. It feels like the right thing to do, and there's laughing, too, lots of laughing. Someone will start telling a Flippa story. Almost always it begins with, "Remember when—"

And then it's all about how the car broke down or it rained on the picnic or the power went out on Christmas Day and the turkey was half-way roasted and it had to be barbecued. Ordinary things. Everyday things. Funny things. Things that went wrong and got put right. Not everything works out for the better. What's wrong with Flippa can't be fixed.

Mom comes tomorrow, and in three hundred and forty-five thousand and six hundred seconds, this last week will be over.

Thursday

Flippa felt better today. She got out of bed. She sat at the kitchen table and drank tea. I had some, too, with plenty of milk and just a bit of sugar. Dad had gone to the airport to pick up Mom. For a whole hour, no one phoned and no one came to visit. For a whole hour, it was just us two.

Flippa said, "I was there when you were born. Did you know that?"

I've always known. How I was born is a story I love to hear. It's a story she loves to tell.

I asked, "What was it like?"

"Miraculous. One minute you weren't there, and the next minute you were, with all your fingers and all your toes, and your eyes wide open. You never cried. You looked around the room. You took us all in. The doctor, the nurses, your father, me. Your mother most of all, of course. She'd worked so hard to set you free."

We sat quietly for one minute, two. I wanted to tell her something, but I wasn't sure how. Finally, I said, "You were there when I was born. And now I'm here for you."

"For when I'm set free," she said.

Flippa looked out to her balcony. There are some tomato plants growing there, heavy with green fruit.

She said, "I'm sorry I won't get to taste this year's tomatoes."

I lost it, then. She held me tight. Her arms are very thin. That's how Mom and Dad found us when they came through the door.

Seconds remaining: two hundred fifty-nine thousand two hundred.

Friday

This is the last day for visitors. They've come in a steady stream. Church friends, bookclub friends, a cousin from California, neighbor after neighbor, all coming to say hello. To say goodbye.

"Please just stay a few minutes," my mom tells them. She's a doctor and knows how to make people pay attention. It's a good thing she's here to take charge. Dad is a mess.

The last to come is Mr. Bark. He's the greengrocer from down the street. Flippa has been buying fruit and vegetables from him for years and years. They always joke when they see each other.

She says, "Now, listen here, Bark. Something is wrong with those plants you sold me. There's not a ripe tomato on them."

Mr. Bark says, "Complain, complain, complain. All you ever do is complain. None of my other customers complain as much as you."

Then they laugh and laugh. Then they hug. Then they say goodbye. Then no more visitors come.

For the next one hundred seventy-two thousand eight hundred seconds, there'll be just us.

Saturday

Dr. Mom sat with Dad and me and Flippa and explained exactly what will happen. Tomorrow, Sunday, at 11, Flippa's doctor will come. She'll give Flippa some medicine to help her relax. She'll give Flippa some medicine to make her sleep. And then, she'll give Flippa the third medicine.

"Will it hurt?" I asked.

"No," said Mom. "It's very gentle."

"Does it hurt now?" I asked.

"Yes," said Flippa. "Now, it hurts."

She needed to rest. I put on her flippers and her goggles. I walked down to the beach. I stood at the ocean's edge. The water stretched on forever. Some people pointed and laughed. What did I care? I was the creature from the Black Lagoon. Who were they?

Flippa was awake when I came back.

"Come here, darling monster," she said, and I snuggled beside her on the bed. The flippers looked funny on the blankets. I liked how the goggles made everything go foggy.

Flippa said, "Ask me anything."

I thought for a long time. I said, "Are you sure?"

She didn't need to think.

"Yes," she said. "Very sure."

It was all I needed to know. In eighty-six thousand and four hundred seconds, the last week will be over.

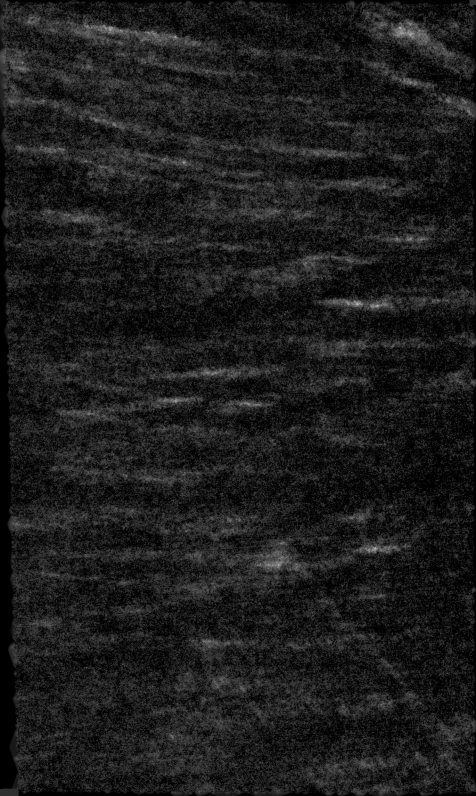

Sunday

I got up early. I was the first to wake. I went onto the balcony. The sky was remembering how to be blue. There were no clouds. I watched the sun rise over the other buildings. Its light was warm on my face. When I turned to go inside, I saw it. There, on the vine, red as the rising sun, shining out from behind the green tangle of leaves, was one small, perfectly ripe tomato. I felt like I should say "Thank you," so I did, to whoever needed to hear. I picked what needed picking. I went inside. I took Flippa her goodbye gift.

Learn More about Assisted Dying

When a person has an illness that will cause their body to die, they can ask a doctor for help. Sometimes, the doctor can use medications or other treatment tools (such as radiation therapy or surgery) that can help the person feel a little better for a little longer. The person who is sick may want to wait to see how much relief they get from their symptoms. Other times, they might ask the doctor or a nurse practitioner to help them to die a little sooner in order to end their suffering, or to be sure they are not alone when they die but surrounded instead by the people they love. This is called an assisted death. Because a medical professional is involved, assisted dying does not hurt.

Knowing someone you love is asking for an assisted death can be confusing, but just as you know your own thoughts and feelings best, so do the people who make this choice for themselves. No one can ever be forced to make this decision, and not many people ever will. It takes great courage to ask for help. In fact, there are a lot of rules around who can ask for this care and how the doctor can help them.

When someone you love makes the decision to have an assisted death, you might feel a variety of emotions. You might be angry because you want them to choose to stay with you. You might wonder why the doctor can't make your loved one better. You might be sad your loved one is dying but happy when you remember all the good memories you share. All of these thoughts are normal, and you're probably not the only one feeling this way. It can feel good to share your feelings with another person who cares for you—a parent, an aunt or uncle, a neighbor, teacher, or a good friend.

You might be asked if you want to be with your loved one when they die. You can be. Or, it might seem too difficult, and you might not want to be present. You can always say goodbye a little earlier and consider leaving a small gift to remind your loved one you are with them in heart. Whatever you decide, you should feel free to ask the assisted dying doctor, your own doctor, or your parents any questions about what will happen. Or visit the links below with a trusted adult.

FOR PARENTS

Contrary to our instinct to protect children, research has shown that children who have more end-of-life information have less anxiety, better trust in health-care professionals and better psychological well-being.

A number of resources can provide more information about kids' grief. Two I recommend are:

1. KidsGrief.ca, offered by Canadian Virtual Hospice.
   In particular, parents can refer to Module 2, "Talking about Dying and Death," Chapter 7, "Preparing for a medically assisted death."

2. Dougy Center (www.dougy.org)
   The National Grief Center for Children & Families (USA)

— Dr. Stefanie Green, co-founder and president of the Canadian Association of MAiD (Medical Assistance in Dying) Assessors and Providers

Last Week was written during a 2019 residency at the University of Manitoba. The author would like to thank Dr. Warren Cariou, Dr. Jocelyn Thorpe, and the Centre for Creative Writing and Oral Culture.

Published in 2022 by Groundwood Books / House of Anansi Press
groundwoodbooks.com

Groundwood Books respectfully acknowledges that the land on which we operate is the Traditional Territory of many Nations, including the Anishinabeg, the Wendat and the Haudenosaunee. It is also the Treaty Lands of the Mississaugas of the Credit.

We gratefully acknowledge for their financial support of our publishing program the Canada Council for the Arts, the Ontario Arts Council and the Government of Canada.

Canada Council
for the Arts

Conseil des Arts
du Canada

ONTARIO ARTS COUNCIL
CONSEIL DES ARTS DE L'ONTARIO
an Ontario government agency
un organisme du gouvernement de l'Ontario

With the participation of the Government of Canada
Avec la participation du gouvernement du Canada | Canadä

Library and Archives Canada Cataloguing in Publication

Title: Last week / written by Bill Richardson ; illustrated by Emilie Leduc.
Names: Richardson, Bill, author. | Leduc, Emilie, illustrator.
Identifiers: Canadiana (print) 20210230096 | Canadiana (ebook) 20210230258 |
ISBN 9781773065663 (hardcover) | ISBN 9781773065670 (EPUB) |
ISBN 9781773065687 (Kindle)
Classification: LCC PS8585.I186 L37 2022 | DDC jC813/.54—dc23

The illustrations were created digitally.
Edited by Karen Li
Designed by Marijke Friesen
Printed and bound in Canada

Groundwood Books is a Global Certified Accessible™ (GCA by Benetech) publisher. An ebook version of this book that meets stringent accessibility standards is available to students and readers with print disabilities.

Groundwood Books is committed to protecting our natural environment. This book is made of material from well-managed FSC®-certified forests, recycled materials, and other controlled sources.

MIX
Paper from
responsible sources
FSC® C016245